THE GHOST OF CAPTAIN BRIGGS

MARY LABATT

KIDS CAN PRESS

Kids Can Press acknowledges the financial support of the Ontario Arts Council, the Canada Council for the Arts and the Department of Cultural Heritage.

Published in Canada by
Kids Can Press Ltd.
29 Birch Avenue
Toronto, ON M4V 1E2

Published in the U.S. by
Kids Can Press Ltd.
4500 Witmer Estates
Niagara Falls, NY 14305-1386

Edited by Charis Wahl and Rivka Cranley
Designed by Marie Bartholomew
Typeset by Karen Birkemoe
Printed and bound in Canada

CM   99 0 9 8 7 6 5 4 3 2 1
CM PA   99 0 9 8 7 6 5 4 3 2

Canadian Cataloguing in Publication Data

Labatt, Mary
    The ghost of Captain Briggs

(Sam, dog detective)
ISBN 1-55074-638-3 (bound)   ISBN 1-55074-636-7 (pbk.)

I. Title. II. Series: Labatt, Mary. Sam, dog detective.

PS8573.A135G46 1999   jC813'.54   C99-931528-5
PZ7.L1155Gh 1999

Kids Can Press is a Nelvana company

To my daughter, Katharine,
Who used to be scared of old houses,
With my love

1. Sam Has a Problem

START PLANNING. I'M DESPERATE.

Jennie Levinsky had an amazing secret. And nobody knew about it except her best friend, Beth Morrison.

It was a warm, summer evening in Woodford, and Jennie was sitting on her back steps. She hugged her knees and thought about her secret. It was the best thing in her life.

As she watched the shadows creep across the quiet backyards, Jennie felt so happy she giggled. Suddenly a voice interrupted her thoughts.

What are you so happy about? My life is wrecked! Trudging around the corner of the house came Sam.

Jennie laughed. "I was just thinking about you!"

With a thud, the huge sheepdog flopped on the ground. Her long white hair drooped over her eyes. *Disaster!* she groaned. *Joan and Bob hate me.*

Sam was Jennie's secret. Everybody knew Jennie had a job walking Sam. And everybody knew Jennie and Beth spent a lot of time with Sam. But no one knew that Jennie could hear what Sam was thinking. Sam's thoughts rang in Jennie's head like a hollow echo. It was just like talking, only it wasn't out loud.

Jennie would never forget the first day Sam talked to her. They were having a picnic when she heard Sam say that she wouldn't drink creek water. Staring at her Sam said, *I knew you'd be able to hear me. Most dogs are too stupid to notice when someone has the gift.* From that moment on, Sam talked to Jennie all the time. It was their secret.

Jennie leaned forward, her long brown hair falling around her face. "What's the matter, Sam?" Jennie's voice was soft.

First I threw up on the couch. The hair over Sam's eyes moved up and down. *That was their fault. They made me eat a can of Liver Delight. Any normal person would throw up after a nice dinner of cat guts.*

Sam heaved an enormous sigh. *Now they're wrecking my life.*

"What are they doing?"

It's all because of that stupid cake. Like a mountain of fur, Sam rolled onto her side and snuffled. *It's not fair.*

Jennie eyed her friend suspiciously. "Did you steal some cake?"

Sam sniffed again. *I did not steal cake. I merely took a few small licks.*

"Aha!" cried Jennie. "You ruined their cake."

Sam was offended. *They shouldn't be so selfish. There was enough icing on that cake for everybody.*

Jennie's gentle face broke into a huge grin. Sam was outraged. *Joan and Bob don't deserve a beautiful dog like me.*

"What happened next, Sam?" Jennie's brown eyes twinkled.

They're sending me to obedience school.

"What's obedience school?"

Sam raised her big head sadly. *It's a place where they torture dogs. You sleep in a doghouse. You eat dry dog food. They shout orders at you all day.*

"Sounds bad."

Sam heaved another sigh. *It's worse than bad. They yank your collar and drag you around. I don't know why the police allow it.*

"Why are Joan and Bob sending you there?"

I told you. They hate me.

"They don't hate you. They must have a reason for sending you."

They're going on a trip and they don't want me. Sam settled her chin on her paws. *They're over there yelling about discipline. They say I'm out of control.*

Jennie hid a smile behind her hand. "Discipline, huh?"

Sam snorted. *They should know better. I don't allow discipline.*

"I don't think you have a choice."

Sam shot Jennie a nasty look. *Of course I do. I'm*

running away on August first.

"I suppose obedience school starts on August second."

Forget obedience school.

"What are you going to do?"

Sam stood up and shook herself. *I'll do what cats do. They sit at somebody's door until they get adopted.*

Jennie shook her head. "It won't work. Joan and Bob would take you back."

Sam slumped back to the ground. *You and Beth are always writing stuff. Write a letter to the Humane Society. This is cruelty to animals.*

"People think its good to train a dog."

Maybe I'll go live in the woods.

Jennie tried to look hopeful. "We'll think of something. We've got two weeks before obedience school starts. All we need is a plan."

Start planning then. I'm getting desperate.

2. Jennie's Brilliant Plan

At dinner the next day, Jennie's parents had news.

"We've found a huge house on Lake Ontario to rent for our vacation," her dad said. "It was built a hundred and fifty years ago by a sea captain."

"We've rented it for the first ten days in August," added Jennie's mother happily. "It'll be a great vacation. We leave in two weeks."

Jennie's older brother groaned. "Don't make me go," Noel whined. "Myrna will find another boyfriend if I go away."

"That would be very smart of Myrna," muttered Jennie. Then she had a thought. Here is the answer to Sam's problem! Sam and Beth had to come on this vacation. It would solve everything.

While they cleared the table, Jennie talked to her mother and father. They said it was a nice idea for Jennie to dog-sit Sam while Joan and Bob were away. Then Jennie asked if she could invite Beth too. She held her breath.

"Why not?" her father laughed. "The more the merrier! Noel can bring a friend too."

Noel called his friends, but they all had plans. "I can't go by myself," he moaned, running his fingers through his spiky blond hair.

But everybody was too busy to listen. Jennie's mother and father were talking about who would run the drugstore while they were away. Jennie ignored Noel because she was busy with her own plans.

Beth's parents agreed to let her come, and Joan and Bob said dog-sitting was a wonderful idea. Jennie, Beth and Sam were ecstatic.

Ha! chortled Sam as she danced around Jennie's bedroom later that week. *I'll sleep on your bed every night. You'd better not snore.*

"Don't get pushy, Sam," warned Jennie as she looked for her bathing suit. "Mom and Dad won't want dogs on beds."

Beth was writing a list of things to pack. She looked up curiously. "Does Sam want to sleep on your bed?"

Jennie nodded. "Yup."

Sam nudged Jennie. *How about a snack?* Jennie was rooting through her drawers. "Now she's hungry." Jennie sorted shorts and T-shirts into two neat piles.

Beth laughed. Her bright red hair shone in the sunlight from the window. "Don't try giving her dog biscuits. It'll start a war. Get her something she likes."

Sam stared at Jennie through the hair over her eyes. *I need something good. How about watermelon with ketchup?*

Beth watched them wistfully. "I wish I could hear Sam. What does she want?"

"You won't believe it — watermelon with ketchup."

Beth giggled. "Yuck!" She patted Sam's big head. "You are a disgusting dog." Sam slurped at her face.

When Jennie got back from the kitchen, both girls watched in amazement as Sam gobbled down the ketchup watermelon.

Sam spat the seeds out on the bedroom floor. *Ptooh! I hate seeds.*

"Stop that! You'll have to clean up," cried Jennie.

Sam spewed seeds onto the bed. *Dogs don't clean up. Everyone knows that.*

Jennie sighed. "You'd better behave on this holiday."

Of course I'll behave. Sam sprayed seeds on the dresser. *I always behave.*

Beth looked up from her packing list. "What did she say?"

"She says she always behaves."

Beth's tiny face lit up. She threw back her head and laughed. Her small nose crinkled and her green eyes sparkled.

Sam eyed her coldly.

"I mean it, Sam." Jennie tried to sound firm. "My parents are in a great mood right now, but it might not last."

Phooey. Everyone loves me. I'm beautiful. I'm smart. And I'm perfect.

"Beth," said Jennie, "you might be interested to know that this dog is beautiful, smart and perfect."

Beth hooted.

3. Meet Mrs. Briggs

At last it was time to leave. The Levinsky's car was full, so Beth's parents said they'd bring her on the weekend. Sam piled in the back seat with Jennie and Noel, and they were on their way.

After three hours the car stopped. Jennie and Sam awoke with a start.

"We're here!" called Jennie's dad. "Now we're really on holiday!"

Jennie looked out the window at the stone mansion. Huge leafy trees towered above a turreted roof. The stained-glass windows, sagging porch and carved door were from another century.

Behind the house, the land fell away to a

hillside of weeds and small bushes. At the bottom of the hill, Lake Ontario shimmered in the sun.

Jennie and Sam clambered out of the car and up the shady walk. The house loomed before them — dark, huge and old. It made Sam think of the stories she loved so much — stories about witches, goblins and ghosts.

"Wow!" breathed Jennie. "It's like a picture out of a book."

What a great house! Sam pranced joyfully beside Jennie. *Mysterious things happen in houses like this. Maybe I can find a mystery in here. My life has been very boring lately.*

When the heavy front door swung open, a strange-looking woman appeared. She had dull hair scraped into a bun, wire-rimmed glasses and lumpy wrinkles. White spikey eyebrows poked out of the top of her spectacles. Without smiling, she stood at the door and waited.

"Hello." Jennie's dad smiled. "We're the Levinsky family. You must be Mrs. Briggs." He climbed the worn stone steps and held out his hand.

Mrs. Briggs didn't move.

Mr. Levinsky dropped his arm. "Well!" he boomed nervously. "Thank you for getting the house ready."

Mrs. Briggs just folded her arms and stared at him.

Who's this crabby old bat? demanded Sam.

"She's the housekeeper," whispered Jennie.

Charming, muttered Sam, rolling her eyes.

Jennie giggled and followed her parents into the house. Everywhere she looked, there were pine floors with homespun rugs, old-fashioned oil lamps and lace curtains.

In the kitchen, black pots hung from ceiling beams. All the bedrooms had high old-fashioned beds. In the bathroom, a high tub stood on feet like a lion's paws.

In the upstairs hall, Jennie noticed a narrow stairway. "What's up there?" she asked.

"The attic," answered her mother.

Sam glanced at the attic door. Along the back

of her neck, she felt the hairs rise. There was something about that door. Sam's heart started to beat a little faster. Here was the promise of adventure and mystery and excitement. Those were the things Sam loved.

Wonderful! Sam chortled as she turned to follow Jennie downstairs. *Somebody is watching us. I'm sure of it.*

4. Sam Smells a Mystery

WONDERFUL! I WON'T BE BORED.

Jennie chose a bedroom with a view of the lake. Jumping up on the bed, Sam put her head on the pillow and yawned.

Jennie heaved her suitcase onto a chair and unzipped it.

Sam opened one eye. *Any food in there?*

"Nope. But Mom and Dad have gone shopping."

Sam's stomach rumbled loudly. After a few minutes, she jumped off the bed. *I'm going to check out the kitchen. I'm starving.*

"Wait for me." Jennie followed Sam into the dim hallway. Behind them, the bedroom door slammed shut. Jennie jumped. She looked up and down the hall, but no one was there. "Noel," she called. But there was no answer.

As she went down the curved staircase, Jennie felt as if someone was watching her. Quickly she whirled around, but there was nothing. Only the closed doors of the silent hall.

Jennie ran down the stairs. "Hey, Sam!" she cried as she rounded the kitchen doorway. "Oof!"

Watch where you're going, grunted Sam.

"What about you? You shouldn't walk off and leave people alone in strange houses!" Jennie looked around.

Oh-ho! You got scared, huh?

"Of course not. Did you find food?"

I forgot I can't open cupboards.

"I'll look." Jennie opened a cupboard. There was no sign of food.

What a stupid house, muttered Sam. *A person could starve in here.*

"There's got to be food somewhere."

Jennie opened every cupboard and drawer. All she found were pots and pans, and neatly stacked dishes. Just as Jennie was opening the last drawer, a long shadow fell over her.

Slowly Jennie looked up.

Staring down at her was Mrs. Briggs. "Just what do you think you're doing?"

"L-l-looking for food," stammered Jennie.

Mrs. Briggs' spectacles glittered. "Do not mess up my kitchen," she said in a hard, flat voice. Her stare bored into Jennie.

Jennie shifted uneasily. "I – I – guess I'll wait for my parents … outside."

Sam and Jennie backed out of the kitchen and ran through the front hall into the sunshine.

"Whew! What a weird person!"

Your parents came to the wrong house.

"No they didn't, Sam. They rented this house for our vacation."

Well somebody better tell that to the General in there.

Jennie twirled a strand of her hair. "I wonder why she's so grumpy."

She's probably hiding something. Sam thought for a moment. *Hiding something … Hmm …*

Sam's spirits soared. *Hiding something is good ... Hey! There's a mystery here!*

Sam forgot that she was hungry. Her head started to buzz with excitement. *We'll find out what Briggsy is hiding. We'll be famous. We'll get our picture in the paper. I take a beautiful picture when I'm brushed. We'll collect a huge reward. We'll be heroes and ...*

Jennie groaned.

5. Strange Digging

HMMM ...
THIS GUY'S GOT
A SECRET!

"What's wrong with Mrs. Briggs?" asked Jennie's mother as she put food in cupboards.

Under the table Sam munched on Jennie's toast. *Fire the old bat.*

"Yeah," said Jennie. "Why don't you fire her?"

"We can't," muttered her dad as he unpacked groceries. "She owns the place."

"She lives in the caretaker's cottage at the edge of the property," added her mom. "She's our housekeeper. That's the agreement."

Sam licked peanut butter from Jennie's spoon. *She's a very spooky housekeeper.*

"I thought having a housekeeper would be a good idea," said Mr. Levinsky glumly.

"It's almost as if she wants us to leave." Jennie's mom stopped putting food away for a moment and stared into space.

"We're not leaving." Her dad was firm. "We've paid for this holiday!"

Nobody is that spooky without a reason. That means the mystery is a good one ... And that means I won't be bored. Boredom is bad.

The next day Jennie and Sam explored the house. Every room was still and silent. When they left Jennie's bedroom, the door slammed behind them again, as if someone had pushed it. Everywhere they went, they felt someone watching them.

They picked their way down the hillside through the bushes and weeds to the lake. When they came out on the beach, Sam was panting. The beach was empty. At one end, a stream emptied into the lake. There was no sign of life. It was like being alone in the world.

"This is a very spooky beach, Sam."

Sam looked around. *I like it. We can bury secret stuff down here.*

"What do you want to bury?"

I don't know yet. But a smart detective always has hiding places ready. Sam smacked her chops. *Open the chips. I'm starved.*

Jennie ripped open the bag and set it on the sand.

Sam nuzzled inside the bag and crunched noisily. *I can't wait to find out the General's secret.*

"I'm not going to tell Noel we think she has a secret. He always laughs at me."

Let him laugh. What does a big lummox like him know?

"What's a lummox?"

An oaf. A fool. A whiny teenager. Have I ever told you how much I hate teenagers?

Jennie giggled. "I think you've mentioned it."

When the chips were gone, Sam and Jennie stretched out on the warm sand and gazed at the clouds.

Suddenly Sam sat bolt upright.

Jennie sat up with a start too. "What is it, Sam?"

I hear something.

Jennie strained to hear. Something was moving on the hillside. She felt nervous on the empty beach. "M-m-maybe we should hide."

Sam looked around. *Good idea. Let's hide in those reeds.*

Without a word they waded into the rushes at the mouth of the stream and crouched down. Sam shuddered. *I hate water.*

A crashing sound came from the bushes. Jennie and Sam peered out between the reeds.

"Ouch!" said a voice. "Stupid prickles!"

The hair over Sam's eyes lifted with interest.

"Yeow!" yelled the voice. "I'm getting stabbed to death!"

A shovel flew out of the underbrush and landed with a thud on the beach.

Sounds like a kid.

Just then an angry boy burst out of the bushes. He had tufty blond hair, freckles and horn-rimmed glasses that sat on the end of his nose. "I hate this!" the boy screamed as he brushed at his long skinny arms furiously.

The boy picked up the shovel and studied a piece of paper. Then he walked over to a spot on the beach and started digging.

"What's he doing?" whispered Jennie.

Who knows? He looks like a very strange kid.

In amazement Sam and Jennie watched as the boy dug a hole, looked at his paper again and started to dig another hole. At last he wiped the sweat from his face, took off his steamy glasses and sat down to rest.

Let's find out what he's doing.

"Wait a minute, Sam."

I want to know! Besides, I have to get out of this revolting water.

"Maybe he's doing something secret."

But Sam crashed through the reeds, on to the beach, and shook herself. Like a sprinkler, she sent water spraying through the air.

"Hey!" shouted the boy, scrambling to his feet.

When Sam finally stopped shaking, she

turned and stared at the reeds. At last Jennie came out.

"Ummm ... er ... h-hello." Jennie felt ridiculous with water streaming from her shorts.

"Where did you two come from?" demanded the boy.

"Umm ... those reeds." Jennie pointed.

"What were you doing in there?" The boy squinted at her.

Jennie's face felt hot. "Oh ... j-just sitting."

Tell him not to be so nosy, said Sam crossly. She bumped Jennie's leg. *Find out why he's digging up the beach.*

"Nobody just sits in water with their clothes on," the boy said suspiciously. "You were spying on me."

Jennie flushed.

The boy picked up his shovel. "I hate spies."

Tell him to buzz off. This is your beach.

"I was not spying," said Jennie. "My parents rented this house."

The boy stopped in his tracks. "So you're the

ones! I heard that someone rented the old Briggs place."

"My name is Jennie Levinsky. This is Sam."

"I'm Liam Collins." He studied Jennie with an odd look for a moment. Then he turned to go back into the bushes.

"So long, Jennie!" he called over his shoulder. "I sure hope you like living in a haunted house."

6. Thuds in the Attic

GHOSTS ARE GREAT!

That night a storm rolled in across the lake. Wind howled and beat at the old house. Huge foamy waves crashed into the hillside. As lightning split the sky, thunder shook the house.

The storm was so fierce that the family huddled together in the living room. Sam wedged herself under a small table beside Jennie, who was crouched in a big chair.

With a bolt of lightning and a crack of thunder, they were plunged into darkness. Jennie couldn't see anything – not even her hand in front of her face.

Jennie clutched Sam. "Mom!" she cried.

Out of the dark came her mother's voice. "We're here, dear."

Sam's low growl filled the room.

Jennie's mom struck a match, and a tiny flame flickered like a pinpoint in the blackness. "I have some candles."

From somewhere in the house came a loud thump.

"What's that?" cried Jennie's mom. The tiny light in her hand shook.

"It sounds like someone's upstairs," her dad said.

"Let's get out of here!" shouted Noel.

Jennie and Sam huddled together. Jennie's eyes were fixed on the light. Another thud. The match jumped and went out.

"Someone's in the attic!" whispered her dad.

Wow! This house really is haunted!

Jennie held on to Sam as her mom lit a candle.

Another thump.

"I want to go home!" whined Noel. "I told you this vacation was stupid."

"I need the candle," said Jennie's dad. "I'm calling the police."

Jennie and Sam heard the sound of the phone being picked up. "The phone's dead!" exclaimed Mr. Levinsky.

"Noel, where's your baseball bat?"

"In the kitchen, by the back door."

"Nobody move. I'll get the bat." As Jennie's dad and the candle bobbed toward the kitchen, the rest of the family was left in darkness again.

"Are you there, Jennie?" Noel's voice seemed very small.

"Yeah." Jennie buried her face in Sam's fur.

"Why are we staying here?" whined Noel.

Thud. Thud. Thud.

It's got to be a ghost! Sam's heart pounded joyfully. *Ghosts are great! You never know what they'll do next.*

The candlelight bobbed to the bottom of the staircase. "Come with me, Noel."

Noel groaned. "Why me?"

"Because you're the biggest," said his dad. "I need your help."

"I'm not the biggest!" cried Noel. "That slobbering pile of fur is bigger than me."

"Good idea. Sam, you come, too," ordered Mr. Levinsky.

"I don't want to stay in the dark without Sam!" cried Jennie.

"Me neither," said her mom. "We're coming, too."

Relax, everybody. I've got great teeth. In Sam's mind, she saw a wispy white ghost floating around, making thumps to scare them. *This is even better than I thought!* She hummed happily to herself.

"Okay. Let's go." Jennie's father started up the stairs with the candle.

Everyone tried to hang on to everyone else. When the lights suddenly blazed on, they were all stumbling along behind Sam. They blinked in the bright light.

"Good." Jennie's dad blew out the candle and looked around. "Whoever you are," he called, "we want you out of here!"

When they got to the attic door, they all

stopped. Jennie's father turned the knob and flung open the door. Darkness.

Gripping the bat, he reached in and felt for the switch. "I hope there's a light …" Everyone waited.

They heard the click of a switch, and light flooded the attic. Lamps, broken furniture, picture frames, boxes and trunks were everywhere. Cobwebs crisscrossed the roof beams. Old white curtains hung crookedly over the window.

"Get out of our house!" yelled Mr. Levinsky into the attic.

Not a sound.

Holding their breath, the family huddled in the doorway as he looked behind furniture and boxes.

"There's nobody here," he said in a puzzled voice. "Noel, come with me. We'll search this house from top to bottom."

Everyone but Sam turned to go downstairs. *I'll watch for a little while,* she told Jennie.

Long after the family had searched the house,

Sam was still watching the attic. Bits of conversation drifted up to her. "It must have been this open window!" they cried. "It was banging in the wind!"

Suddenly Sam cocked her head. From behind the attic door came a stealthy shuffling sound.

Sam's head buzzed with excitement. *It isn't the window. It's a ghost. A spine-chilling, hair-raising, wonderful ghost!* Sam chortled. *I love it. People will want to hear about this ...*

I wonder if a dog can get on a talk show?

7. All Detectives Get Scared

ANYTHING CAN HAPPEN IN A HAUNTED HOUSE!

When Jennie awoke the next morning, Sam was staring at her. *That kid on the beach was right. This house is haunted, Jennie. I heard more noises in the attic last night. Terrible things can happen in haunted houses. People die. Dogs disappear.*

"That's really scary." Jennie blinked.

Phooey! All the best things in life are scary. Sam stared harder. *Follow me. I'll show you.*

Reluctantly Jennie got up out of bed and followed Sam. Sam shoved through the door, ignored it when it slammed and dashed up the attic stairs. At the attic door, she stopped and waited for Jennie to turn the doorknob.

But Jennie couldn't touch the knob. "I – I'm

too scared, Sam."

Don't be silly. Sam pawed at the door. Suddenly she stopped in mid-scratch. *Did you hear that?* Sam poked Jennie with her round nose. *Something's moving in there!*

Jennie put her ear to the door and listened. From behind the door came small scratching sounds.

Open it, ordered Sam. *Wait! Get a camera. We need proof.*

Jennie gasped. "You want me to walk in there and take a picture of a ghost?"

Of course. How else can we prove it?

A ghostly sound echoed through the door.

Cre-e-eak ...

Sam wiggled happily.

Jennie turned pale. "I – I don't want to see a ghost, Sam."

Cre-e-eak ...

Sam held her breath as she listened to the small, secret sound. It spoke of dark nights and hidden things. Hairs prickled deliciously up and down her spine.

Cre-e-eak …

"Let's go, Sam," whispered Jennie. "I'm not going in there."

Don't be a wimp, Jennie. This is our big chance. We might not get this close to a ghost again.

But Jennie was running down the stairs.

With a sigh, Sam followed. *Phooey.*

8. Who Was Captain Briggs?

THIS GETS BETTER AND BETTER!

It was Saturday. Beth was coming that afternoon!

Jennie decided to ride her bike into the village with Sam. "I can't just sit here and wait for Beth," she said. "Somebody's watching us."

It's the ghost. Ghosts always watch people.

When they got to the village, a bike skidded to a stop beside them. It was the boy they had met on the beach. His horn-rimmed glasses hung crookedly on the end of his nose.

"You're the kid from the old Briggs house," he said.

Jennie smiled. "And you're Liam Collins. You were digging on the beach."

Liam didn't smile back. "So, Jennie ... how do you like living with a ghost?"

"Are you sure the house is haunted?" Jennie sounded worried.

"Of course I'm sure. Ask anybody in town."

What did I tell you!

Liam peered at Jennie. "Why did you move into that house? Nobody around here would live in it."

Jennie scuffed the grass with the toe of her running shoe. "Who's the ghost?" she asked nervously.

"A sea captain, Percival Albert Briggs."

Jennie's mouth felt dry. "The captain who built the house?"

Liam snorted. "He wasn't just a sea captain. He was a pirate!"

Jennie's hand flew to her mouth.

Liam eyed her narrowly. "And a murderer. Are you sure you don't know about him?"

This gets better and better by the minute.

"How could we know? Nobody told us!" squeaked Jennie.

Liam shook his head. "Everyone knows about that ghost." He stood up on his bike pedals and was gone.

"Why didn't someone tell my parents?" Jennie cried to Liam's disappearing back.

A picture of fierce pirates popped into Sam's mind.

"Wait until my parents find out that house was built by a pirate." Shakily, Jennie climbed back on her bike.

In her mind, Sam watched pirates swarm over their anchored ship. Some of them scrambled up the ship's rigging. Others loaded heavy chests into the hold. Some of the pirates had eye patches and earrings. Their faces were cruel.

Chests, thought Sam. *Hmm ... now that's something I didn't think about ... but I know what it means!* Sam watched the scene unfold. *Where there are chests there's got to be treasure.*

Sam ran beside Jennie's bike humming happily to herself. *We'll find Captain Briggs' pirate treasure. And we'll get a reward ... We're going to be famous ... And rich ... Rich is good ... Famous is excellent.*

When Jennie didn't answer, Sam looked up at her curiously. *Are you listening?*

Jennie shuddered. "Of course I'm listening. We're going to find his pirate treasure and we're going to be famous."

Right. And rich. What's wrong with that?

"Nothing, if you like taking treasure from a fierce ghost."

9. A Nasty Surprise

Beth arrived that afternoon. As soon as Beth's parents left, Jennie and Sam hustled her up to Jennie's room. The door slammed behind them. Jennie jumped. Beth looked puzzled.

Jennie stood with her back to the door. "Beth, get ready for a shock."

Leaping onto the bed, Sam danced merrily. *I love this.* As she danced, she whipped the quilt into little swirls.

"What?" asked Beth. Her small body was tense with curiosity.

"You have to promise you won't get mad," begged Jennie.

Beth looked surprised. "Why would I get mad?"

"Well …" Jennie glanced at Sam. "What if a friend let you come to a dangerous place?" Jennie chewed her lip. "Would you be mad?"

Beth shrugged. "I guess so."

Never mind about that, snapped Sam. *Tell her about the mystery.*

"I am telling her, Sam," said Jennie. "You be quiet."

Beth grinned and kissed the top of Sam's big head. "Still giving Jennie orders, I see. You are so weird, Sam."

Sam chuckled and stared at Jennie. *Hurry up and tell her.*

"Okay. It's like this, Beth," Jennie began nervously. "I know I should have phoned you …"

Tell her! Sam stood on the bed and scowled.

Jennie gulped. "Beth …" She took a deep breath and clasped her hands together. "Beth … there's a ghost here."

Beth jumped. "A ghost?"

"Yeah, a ghost."

Not just an ordinary ghost, crowed Sam. *A bloodthirsty, dangerous ghost. The ghost of a murdering pirate. A pirate who has a huge treasure buried somewhere around here.* As Sam danced about, her long fur floated around her. She caught sight of herself in the mirror and stopped for a moment to admire her reflection.

"Sam, we don't know if he buried a treasure," said Jennie. "And stop messing up my bed."

"Treasure?" Beth was furiously biting her fingernails. "Why would a ghost have a treasure?"

"Because he's a pirate, Beth."

"A pirate?" Beth was wide-eyed.

"A boy named Liam told us the ghost is Captain Briggs. He was a pirate – and a murderer."

"Murderer?"

Sam glared at Beth. *Stop repeating everything.*

"Wow," said Beth, sinking down on the crumpled bed. "I've never been in a haunted house. How do you know there's a ghost here?"

"We heard him," answered Jennie.

Tell her about the thumping, said Sam.

"There were some thuds in the attic during a

storm," said Jennie. "My parents think it was a window banging, but we think it came from the attic."

Tell her about the other sound we heard.

"Sam and I heard different sounds through the attic door."

Tell her about the creaking.

"And there was creaking in there."

Sam flopped on the bed. *You take three hours to tell a simple fact. Where's the popcorn?*

Sam hopped off the bed and snuffled around underneath it until she found an open popcorn bag. Then she lay down to lap it up.

Beth looked around the room. "Are you scared?"

"Really scared," admitted Jennie. "This is a spooky house. Wait until you see the housekeeper. Her name is Briggsy and she hates us."

Forget about her. I want to get a look at this ghost. And I'm going to find his pirate treasure. Sam chomped popcorn loudly. *It's a good thing I am a great detective.*

"Sam wants to see the ghost. And she wants to find his treasure," said Jennie. "She's over there bragging about how smart she is."

"I thought you weren't sure about the treasure."

"Well, Sam keeps saying a pirate has to have buried treasure."

Pirates always have treasure. Everybody knows that.

All night the old house creaked and groaned with ghostly noises. When Jennie and Beth woke up, they were glad to see daylight. As they were getting dressed, they noticed that a folded paper had been slipped under the bedroom door.

"What's this?" Jennie unfolded the paper. It was a note.

What is it? asked Sam sleepily.

Jennie didn't answer.

"Let me see." Beth reached for the note.

Silently Jennie handed it to Beth.

"Oh no!"

Sam jostled Jennie's leg. *What is it?*

Jennie and Beth just stared at the paper.

Tell me! insisted Sam. *You know I hate reading.*

"Read it out loud, Beth," said Jennie.

Beth slowly read the large black words.

"GO HOME NOW."

10. The Story of One-Eye

I HOPE HE COMES TO VISIT.

When Jennie, Beth and Sam left the bedroom, the door slammed behind them.

"It's him!" screamed Jennie, hanging on to Beth.

They ran downstairs and out the front door.

"Who do you think wrote that note?" Beth's green eyes were huge.

The ghost wrote it. Ghosts don't want people in their houses.

"Sam says the ghost wrote it," said Jennie. "I wonder what my parents would say about this."

Don't show them yet! They'll take us home! I want to get a look at this ghost.

"Sam thinks if Mom and Dad see this note,

they'll make us go home. She wants to see the ghost."

Beth looked worried. "It'll be scary."

Really scary, chuckled Sam. *Maybe he'll come into our room while we're sleeping. Then I'll see him!*

Jennie clapped her hands over her ears. "Stop, Sam! I don't want a ghost in our room!"

Beth chewed her fingernail. "Let's go to the library and find out about this."

Inside the library, they went to the information desk.

"Can I help you?" the librarian asked brightly, her blue eyes crinkling in a friendly way. "My name is Mrs. Potts."

Jennie explained that they were doing research. "We would like to know about Captain Percival Albert Briggs," she said politely. "He built the old house at the edge of town."

Mrs. Potts' eyes narrowed. "Somebody rented that house."

"It's my family," said Jennie. "We'd like to know the history of the house."

"You are living in that house?" Mrs. Potts asked in a curious voice.

Jennie nodded.

Mrs. Potts gave them an odd look. "Well ... we have a section on local history. Follow me." She cast a worried look at Sam. "You can bring your dog if it behaves." She turned to Sam. "If you don't behave, you're out."

Sam gasped. *I know how to behave in a library. I am a very intelligent dog.* She glared at Mrs. Potts. *Everyone loves me.*

Mrs. Potts did not notice Sam's angry look. "This way."

The three friends watched Mrs. Potts run her finger along the shelves. Finally she took down a book. "This is a history of the old houses in the area." She flipped through the pages.

"Here it is." She held out a picture of a bearded man in old-fashioned clothes. "Here is a drawing of Captain Briggs."

One beady cruel eye blazed from the page.

The other eye was covered with a patch. Bushy black whiskers framed a brutal face.

"He looks scary," said Beth.

Sam pushed to the front. *I can't see.*

"Wait, Sam," said Jennie. "We'll let you see in a minute."

Mrs. Potts looked surprised.

Sam scowled at the librarian. *Get out of my way. First you insult me and then you ignore me.*

"Are you sure this dog behaves?" Mrs. Potts raised her eyebrows at Jennie.

"She's no trouble at all!" sang Jennie, poking Sam in the ribs.

"I hope you're right," Mrs. Potts said with a suspicious look at Sam. Then she was gone.

Sitting down in a corner with Sam wedged between them, the girls leaned over the book eagerly.

Beth gasped. "He was a famous pirate! He was called One-Eye because he wore a patch."

"He was born in Bristol, England, in 1804," read Jennie.

Beth read a few lines. "He was wanted for

robbing ships ... And he was wanted for murder!"

"Look!" Jennie pointed. "His ship sank in a storm in Lake Ontario in 1849!"

"Yeah. And it says here his body was never found. Neither was his treasure."

Beth furrowed her brow and read. "He had hideouts along the St. Lawrence River. He was the only pirate who sailed into Lake Ontario."

Jennie chewed her lip and read furiously. "Beth, he built a house near Fernley! He was trying to get home when his ship sank."

They looked at each other. "A house near Fernley!" breathed Beth. "That's where we are!"

Beth and Jennie stared at the picture in horror.

Captain Briggs was a thief and a murderer, and they were trapped in a house with him.

11. A Mysterious Map

I KNEW THERE WAS A TREASURE.

As Jennie put the book back, a paper fluttered to the floor. Beth picked it up.

Sam peered over Beth's shoulder. *A treasure map!*

"Give me that," said a nasty voice.

Turning around, they saw Liam's tufty head rounding the bookshelves. He grabbed for the map, but Beth was too quick for him. She hopped on a chair.

"Give me that!" hissed Liam. "It's mine."

Sam growled menacingly.

"Go away," whispered Jennie. "It's not yours. It was in the book."

"It's mine." Liam grabbed at the crumpled

map, but Beth raised it higher.

Sam bared her fangs and growled louder.

All around the library, people looked up in amazement.

"Just one minute!" roared a voice. Bearing down on them in full fury came Mrs. Potts. She pointed at the door. "Get that dog out of here!"

Sam bared her fangs and snapped at Mrs. Potts. *I'm not the problem. Throw that weird-looking kid out.*

Mrs. Potts gasped. "Don't you dare snap at me!"

Sam growled instead.

Mrs. Potts glared at Sam. "If you growl again, I'll hit you with this book."

Sure you will. People don't hit me with books, lady. Everyone loves me. "Grrrrr."

Wham! Mrs. Potts smacked Sam over the head with the book.

Sam reeled.

"There," said Mrs. Potts firmly. "In my library, everyone behaves. Now get out!"

Jennie and Beth skulked through a sea of

staring faces. Sam walked proudly behind, thinking terrible thoughts about Mrs. Potts and terrible thoughts about libraries.

She's just lucky I didn't tear her to shreds. She took a big chance when she tangled with me.

At the library door, Sam decided to treat everybody to one last growl. *Ouch,* she winced. *That hurts my head. I'll growl later.*

As Jennie, Beth and Sam went down the stairs, mutters and whispers followed them. Grumbling complaints about kids and dogs tumbled out the library door.

Sam chuckled. *Looks like we started something.*

When the three friends got to the street, they heard a yell. Turning around, they saw Liam running toward them, his angry face beet red. "Hand over my map!"

Quickly Beth put her hand over the pocket where she had stuffed the map. She stuck out her small chin and stared up at Liam. "How do we know it's your map?"

"It just is!" shouted Liam, towering over Beth. He rammed his glasses back up on his nose. "I read that book and I made that map. Hand it over!"

Sam's headache suddenly disappeared. *I told you there's a treasure! That's why he's digging up the beach! He knows there's pirate treasure.* She pushed Jennie's leg. *Ask him. Ask him. Hurry up.*

"You think Captain Briggs buried his pirate treasure on our beach, don't you?" asked Jennie.

Liam just scowled at her.

"We want to find the treasure, too," said Beth.

Liam gave them a very strange look.

"We could work together," suggested Jennie hopefully.

Sam's head whipped up. *Share the loot? Not on your life. Let's go.*

In a flash Liam snatched the paper out of Beth's pocket and was gone.

12. A Door

Later that afternoon, the three friends picked their way through the underbrush down to the beach.

Jennie held her nose with one hand. With the other, she tried to hold a bag and a shovel. "These sardine sandwiches really stink, Sam."

I need food, don't I?

"The next time you want something this smelly, you can carry it yourself," Jennie grumbled.

I suppose you want me to starve.

Just then they popped out of the underbrush onto the empty beach. The water was perfectly still.

"Wow!" Beth looked up and down the beach. "It's really lonely here."

A strong puff of wind tugged at their clothes and whipped the hair off Sam's eyes. Instantly the beach was still again.

Jennie looked around. "What was that?"

It's the ghost. Sam snickered. *He wants us off the beach.*

Nervously, they waited for another gust of wind, but it didn't come.

"So ... those are the holes Liam's been digging," said Beth finally.

Jennie gazed into an empty hole. "Let's get started. Maybe we'll find something."

With the wonderful smell of sardines wafting across her nose, Sam lay down to watch the work. Jennie and Beth poked their shovels into the first hole.

Then Sam had a thought. *I know why that ghost is so mad. He doesn't want us to find the treasure.*

"That doesn't make sense." Jennie pushed the shovel deeper into the sand. "Ghosts don't need money."

He's guarding it! Sam started to pace back and forth. *That's why Briggsy is so unfriendly! She works for the ghost!*

"What?"

I think Old One-Eye tells her what to do.

Beth stopped digging. "What's Sam talking about?"

"She thinks the ghost talks to Briggsy." Jennie leaned on her shovel. "Sam thinks the ghost is giving Briggsy orders."

Sam's pink tongue hung out as she panted with excitement. *No wonder the ghost is worried.* She whirled around gleefully. *We're going to snatch the treasure from under his nose!*

Jennie's brown eyes clouded. "He's a ghost, Sam. Ghosts are dangerous."

Sam snorted. *Who cares? I can't wait to see a real ghost. We'll have the treasure. We'll be rich! And famous ... Don't forget famous.*

The girls dug while Sam munched on sardines and lounged in the sun.

At last Beth flopped on the beach. "I can't dig any more," she wheezed.

"Me neither," huffed Jennie, throwing down her shovel. "I give up."

"We'll never find anything."

Sam lumbered to her feet and peered into a hole. *We need a bulldozer.* She hopped down into the hole and sniffed.

Tiredly, Jennie and Beth watched Sam go from hole to hole.

When she got to a hole at the base of the hill, Sam stopped. She cocked her head and sniffed. *What's this?* A musty smell filtered through the sand and pebbles. Sam sniffed again. Stale air, smelling of damp and moss and darkness, wafted into her nostrils. *I've found something!* Sam whipped around. *There's something here!*

Jennie scrambled to her feet. "Sam's found something!"

Smell this!

Jennie ran over and sniffed. "I can't smell anything."

Human noses are useless. Dig here.

"She wants us to dig here, Beth," said Jennie.

The girls dug. There was no sound, only the

scrape, scrape of the shovels.

When a loud clank rang out, Sam jumped. Beth's shovel had hit something!

"It's the treasure!" screamed Jennie, digging wildly.

"We found it!" shouted Beth, sand flying beneath her shovel.

I told you! crowed Sam.

In a frenzy, the girls dug until a streak of gray wood appeared in the hillside. When they scraped the sand away, they saw gray boards.

"It's the side of a wooden chest!" panted Beth.

"We've got to find the lock!" yelled Jennie.

As they worked, the circle of wood grew bigger.

"Here it is!" puffed Jennie, feeling a lump under the sand. She scraped dirt and sand off a thin piece of rusty metal. She looked at it closely. "It doesn't look like a lock."

"Maybe the chest isn't locked," suggested Beth.

Sam stopped dancing and peered over the

edge of the hole. *Maybe it isn't a chest.*

Both girls stared at the latch. It wasn't a chest.

They had found a door in the side of the hill.

13. Should We Go In?

I'M SURROUNDED BY WIMPS.

Suddenly Jennie noticed that the sun was getting lower in the sky. "We have to go home. We don't have time to open the door now!" she cried with relief.

Drat.

Beth was disappointed. "Let's hide it with branches and we'll come back tomorrow."

Double drat. And phooey.

As they scrambled up the hill, Jennie and Beth could feel the ghost breathing down their necks.

In bed that night, both girls clung to Sam. All through the night, the house moaned. They were sure they could hear the ghost muttering,

"Don't you dare open that door. Don't you dare."

When they woke up, they found another note under the door. It was in the same heavy black print as the first one.

Jennie read it aloud: "STOP SNOOPING."

Big deal, snorted Sam. *Send the ghost a note. Tell him we're not scared.*

Shakily, Jennie put the note on the bookshelf with the other one.

Beth chewed on a fingernail. "I think he's getting really mad."

Sam hummed a little tune.

Fearfully, Jennie looked around the room. "He's watching everything we do."

Beth gulped. "Let's go outside."

When the three friends left the bedroom, the door slammed hard. Jennie and Beth shrieked and they all ran downstairs.

When Jennie, Beth and Sam got outside, they

saw Mrs. Briggs watching them from the caretaker's cottage. Spectacles flashing, mouth set in a hard, tight line, she just stared.

"Her face looks strange, doesn't it?" whispered Beth.

Jennie nodded. "Yeah. She doesn't look like a real person."

She isn't a real person, said Sam. *One-Eye Briggs has taken over her body.*

"Sam thinks the ghost has taken over her body."

Beth shuddered. "Let's keep walking."

When they got to the beach, they stepped out of the bushes into familiar stillness. Jennie's heart pounded. Beth's mouth was dry.

Sam danced excitedly at the edge of the hole, as Jennie moved the branches.

"W-w-where could this door go?" Jennie wondered.

"I think it's an underground room." Two bright red spots burned on Beth's cheeks.

Jennie shivered.

Beth squared her small shoulders firmly.

"Let's go to work." She started to scoop dirt and stones away from the door.

When they finished, they had uncovered a small door in the hillside. Weathered gray planks were held fast by a rusty latch.

Sam sniffed a musty smell through the door. *Open it!*

Beth held her breath and reached for the latch. Slowly she lifted it. Jennie felt like she was going to faint.

With a grinding sound, the door opened.

Expecting the ghost to jump out, Jennie covered her head. Nothing happened.

At last Jennie looked up. Stretching deep into the hill was black, mossy, musty darkness.

Sam shoved past the girls and leaned in. She felt the tiniest rush of air. *This is bigger than one room. Maybe it's an underground city.*

"S-S-Sam thinks there's more than just one room," whispered Jennie.

"Pirates had tunnels, didn't they?" Beth whispered. "Maybe it's his tunnel."

Around the doorway they could see stone

walls and a sand floor, but the blackness ahead was thick. They could feel the ghost watching them.

"Sh-sh-should we go in?" Jennie clasped her hands together fearfully.

Sam rolled her eyes. *Of course we should go in.*

"We need flashlights," Beth said suddenly.

"There's one in our room." Jennie backed away from the door. "I'll get it."

Carefully they closed the door.

"Someone should stand guard." Beth flung branches back over the hole to hide the doorway.

"You stay," said Jennie, anxious to get away.

I'll stay, too. Sam flopped on the sand.

"Hurry," urged Beth. "It's really spooky here."

Jennie disappeared into the underbrush, leaving Sam and Beth sitting on the beach.

"The ghost is going to come right out of that hole," Beth whispered and edged closer to Sam. "I know it. I just know it."

Sam sighed.

Wimps. Why do I know so many wimps?

14. Inside the Tunnel

When Jennie came back with the flashlight, Beth was still huddled next to Sam.

As soon as they moved all the branches, they pulled at the edge of the door. With a groan it opened.

Shakily, Jennie shone the flashlight in the doorway. The circle of light wavered across stone walls on every side. For several minutes, they tried to see into the darkness.

"It looks like a tunnel," whispered Jennie.

Sam pushed at their legs. *Let me through. I want to see.*

"Don't push, Sam," hissed Jennie. "We could fall down a hole."

Sam pushed again. *I'm growing old waiting for you two.*

Very slowly Beth placed her foot on the dirt floor inside the tunnel. She carefully put down her other foot and started to walk. The tunnel was silent. Jennie shone the light ahead.

Beth and Jennie held on to each other, the light wobbling in the dark. Sam tried to shove in front of them.

Jennie kept looking around nervously. The floor seemed to be sloping. "W-we're going uphill," she whispered.

Hurry up. I don't see why you two get to go first.

After what seemed like a long time, Beth stopped. Jennie and Sam piled up behind her. "Look back!"

When they turned around, they saw only a small patch of light. Behind them was the beach, the sunshine, everything that was familiar and safe. Ahead of them lay darkness.

"M-m-maybe we should go back out for a m-minute." Jennie's voice faltered.

Without another word, the girls turned and

stumbled back to the light. They felt the ghost reaching for them with bony fingers.

At last they tumbled onto the beach, blinking in the sunlight.

Sam hopped out of the hole and flopped down on the sand. *Why is this taking so long?*

"Stop pressuring us, Sam," said Jennie nervously. "We need to be careful."

Sam rolled her eyes. *I want to see the ghost. Then we'll be careful.*

15. Something's in There

AHA! I KNOW WHAT THAT IS!

For several minutes the girls couldn't move.

"M-m-maybe we should quit," Jennie stammered at last. She looked at Beth. "What do you think?"

Sam was alarmed. *Who's talking about quitting?*

Beth shook her head. "I'm never quitting."

Sam heaved a sigh of relief. *That's better.*

"Well ... okay. I ... I guess we should find the treasure," said Jennie, twisting her hair nervously. "Now that we've started."

Think of how much fun it will be to be rich. Can dogs rent planes? Hotel rooms? Yachts?

In spite of her fears, Jennie smiled. "Sam's talking about being rich. She's planning to rent planes and boats and stuff."

Beth grinned. "Ask her what else she'll do."

I'll start a snack factory. Chocolate cookies with sardine filling. Cheese ice cream. Jelly and tuna doughnuts.

Jennie reached over and rubbed Sam's ear. "She's starting a snack company. Her snacks are gross."

I'll have servants and pizzas. Sam looked dreamily at the sky.

"Now she's talking about servants."

"We'd better stop daydreaming," said Beth. "We need a plan."

Sam lumbered to her feet. *We have a plan.We're going to see the ghost and get his treasure. Come on.*

"Sam says we've got a plan."

Sam hopped down to the doorway. With a little growl, she stepped into the tunnel.

Jennie shrieked, "Sam!" But Sam had disappeared into the darkness.

"We have to go after her." Beth jumped in behind Sam.

Sam was inside the tunnel. *Follow me.*

Jennie shone the flashlight as they inched along the passageway. On and on they went into the dank, stale air. The ground sloped upward. With each step, the air got mustier.

Sam wheezed. *Maybe this is how a ghost smells.*

After a long time, Sam stopped and sniffed. *There's something up ahead.*

Slowly Jennie moved the flashlight in a circle. For the first time, the light caught something. Jennie moved the light across a surface. Boards … hinges … a latch.

It was another door, like the one outside.

Sam crept up to the door and sniffed again. Moldy air choked her. *Agh*, she gagged. *This must be the ghost's room.*

They crept up to the door. Her heart jumping, Jennie shone the light on the latch. With careful fingers, Beth raised it slowly. It moved.

When the door opened, a blast of musty air hit them. Jennie put her arms over her head to protect herself. Beth scrunched her eyes shut in terror. They waited. Nothing happened.

Sam coughed. *Shine the light.*

As the light moved, Jennie and Beth watched fearfully. At any moment they expected to see the wispy shape of the ghost. But they saw only a dirt floor and old stone walls.

"It's a cellar," whispered Jennie.

"It must be under the house," said Beth.

Sam squeezed through the door. *There's got to be something in here. Shine the light around again.*

Jennie moved the flashlight beam around the cellar. "There's nothing here."

Wait! I saw something. Go back.

Jennie moved the light.

"There's something in there!" hissed Beth.

Jennie crisscrossed again.

"Over there." Beth pointed. Something was propped up in the corner.

"What is it?" whispered Jennie.

I know what it is.

Jennie looked at Sam. "What is it, Sam?"

It's a pirate sword!

16. Will One-Eye Come?

PHOOEY.
I'M NEVER
SCARED.

Getting out of the tunnel seemed to take forever. When they stepped on to the beach, a sudden gust of wind whipped their clothes around them.

"Yikes!" screamed Jennie. "It's the ghost! Let's get out of here!"

"Wait for me!" yelled Beth, as she threw branches over the hole to hide the door.

In a tangle of arms and legs, the three friends scrambled up the hill and back to the house.

Giddy with relief, they piled into the bedroom. While Sam pranced on the bed, the girls laughed and giggled and threw pillows.

When they finally slowed down, Jennie got

some cheesy-onion chips and poured cream soda into a bowl. Sam jumped off the bed, ambled over to the bowl and lapped up the pop.

Sam groaned when she saw Beth pick up pencil and paper. *Don't start writing.*

She glared as Beth wrote at the top of the page, How to Find a Ghost.

Beth eyed her title and drew little hearts around it. "Now, what should we do next?"

Sam sighed. *Why does this kid have to write everything down? Writing is a big waste of time. It's almost as bad as reading.*

"I like it when Beth makes lists, Sam," said Jennie. "They keep us organized."

Being organized is another waste of time.

Jennie ignored her. "First, I guess we should look at the sword ... Only, I don't want to go back in the tunnel."

"Shouldn't a cellar have stairs from the house?" Beth chewed her pencil.

"Yeah," said Jennie. "Every basement has stairs."

"Well … that's step one." Beth wrote firmly: Find the cellar stairs.

"Number two." Beth wrote: Search the cellar. She looked up. "What's next?"

The attic is next, you nitwits. And the tunnel. And we have to spy on Briggsy to see when the ghost visits her. Sam slumped down on the bed. *Is this your idea of a good time?*

When Beth finished, she read her list aloud.

1. Find the cellar stairs.
2. Search the cellar.
3. Search the attic.
4. Search the tunnel.
5. Spy on Briggsy to see when the ghost visits her.

When she heard the last one, Sam cheered up a little. *I'm going to love spying on Briggsy. The old bat!*

In Sam's mind, Briggsy stepped out of the dark woods. From the ground in front of her, a mist rose up. Out of the mist stepped a fierce pirate. One-Eye! The moon shone silvery beams over Briggsy as she listened to his orders. Then more mist came up and … Poof! One-Eye was gone.

Jennie had a sudden thought. "The ghost will know we've been in his tunnel. What do you think he'll do?" she asked in a small, squeaky voice.

Sam stopped licking the chip bag. *Try and scare us to death. That's all.*

Beth's face turned white under her flaming red hair. "You don't suppose he'd come after us?"

Jennie gasped. "What if he comes tonight?"

17. A Visit from Captain Briggs

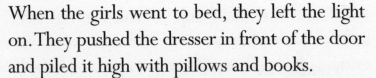

When the girls went to bed, they left the light on. They pushed the dresser in front of the door and piled it high with pillows and books.

"He can still walk through this stuff," panted Beth as she heaped clothes on the dresser.

"I don't care," muttered Jennie, putting her favorite teddy bear on top. "It makes me feel better."

The three friends crawled into bed. Instantly Sam started to snore.

Jennie and Beth lay awake — waiting. Every sound made them jump. After a long while, they looked at the time. Eleven o'clock. The night was going to last forever.

Then they heard it. From above them came a scratching sound.

Shuffle ... Shuffle ... Scratch ... Scratch ...

Jennie yanked the covers over her head. Beth pulled her pajama top over her eyes.

With a start, Sam woke up and growled. Stepping in a bowl of popcorn, she jumped off the bed. *What is it? What's happening?*

Jennie and Beth dove under the covers. "It's the ghost!" wailed Jennie. "He's come to get us."

"What if he's got his sword?" squealed Beth, wriggling to the bottom of the bed.

I'll bite him. Stay calm.

Sam stepped on a piece of pizza that stuck to her foot. As she clumped around the room, the pizza slapped against a can of cola. The can careened across the floor.

Scratch ... Scratch ... Scratch ...

Muffled screams came from the bed.

"Grrrrrrr." Sam bared her fangs at the ceiling.

"Help!" cried the shapes under the blankets.

A low squeaking seemed to come out of the walls.

"He's here!" screamed the lumps in the bed. "Oh, no!"

Barking and growling, Sam leaped on the bed.

"He's got us!" screamed a voice. "Help!"

Barking wildly, Sam jumped up and down, her feet stomping on the writhing bumps under the covers.

"Ouch!"

"Oof!"

At the door, the dresser started to shake. Sam barked louder. *He's coming through the door!*

"Yikes!"

The dresser jiggled.

Here he comes! Get ready!

"Help!"

The dresser wobbled.

He's coming right through the dresser!

"Help! Help!"

The dresser teetered wildly.

"Open the door this minute!" yelled a voice.

"It's One-Eye!" screamed the wriggling shapes on the bed.

"Open this door!" roared a huge voice.

Sam burrowed under the covers with the girls.

The dresser crashed to the floor.

The door flew open.

"Help!"

"Grrrrrr."

"What is going on in here?"

"Help!"

The blankets were pulled off the three humps. Jennie and Beth covered their heads and screamed.

"Grrrrrr."

"Don't you dare growl at me!" Jennie's father glared at Sam.

Sam was going to growl again, but she remembered Mrs. Potts in the library. She shut her mouth instantly.

"What's going on here?" Mr. Levinsky's face was beet red.

"What have you done to this room?" Mrs. Levinsky looked at the mess in horror.

Noel peered around the doorway. "You kids

are crazy. I never did anything like this when I was your age."

"Get out of that bed this minute and tell us what is going on." Jennie's dad was turning a bright shade of purple.

Meekly the three climbed out of bed.

"Just what is the meaning of this?" Jennie's mom folded her arms and waited.

Tell them, Jennie. Or they'll keep yelling.

"It's – it – it's the ghost," stammered Jennie.

"Ghost!" cried her dad. "What ghost? There is no such thing as a ghost!"

Jennie gulped. "He was scratching on our ceiling."

"And moving around up there," Beth added. "We heard him moving in the attic."

"There is no ghost," repeated Jennie's mom.

"But we heard him squeaking," Jennie objected.

"The dresser wobbled," said Beth timidly.

"Of course it did!" cried Mrs. Levinsky. "We were trying to get in, to see what you were shouting about."

Noel guffawed and fell back on the bed. When he sat up, a slice of pizza was stuck to his hair.

Looks good on you.

"You girls have to clean this room," said Jennie's mom firmly. "I want it spotless." Then she softened. "I promise you, there are no ghosts. We'll talk about this in the morning."

Jennie's dad tried to smile. "Really, girls, there's no ghost. It's an old house and it just seems spooky."

At the door he turned around. "This mess has to be cleaned up before Mrs. Briggs comes in the morning."

Getting through the rest of the night was no fun. Sam sprawled on the bed and watched the girls work. *I can't understand why everyone gets mad at us.*

"Yeah," grunted Jennie, prying a bit of pizza off a pillow. "We heard the ghost. They just don't believe us."

"I've read about this," said Beth glumly. "Grown-ups don't listen, and the kids get killed. At the funeral they're all crying, but it's too late."

You think nobody listens to kids? You should try being a dog. Sam pulled two pillows off the bed and dragged them to a corner.

"They'll listen when we find the treasure," Jennie said.

Noel will beg us to buy him something, muttered Sam.

As the girls were picking up the last bits of pizza, they spied a crumpled paper near the door. Jennie grabbed it. When she read it, her hand flew to her mouth.

Sam looked up. *I bet I know what that is.*

"It's another note!"

"What does it say this time?" Beth asked in a hollow voice.

"It says, 'YOU'LL BE SORRY.'"

18. Trapped in the Darkness

SO NOBODY'S PERFECT.

The next morning, Jennie hopped out of bed. "Mom and Dad need to see those notes. That'll prove there's a ghost."

When she went to the bookshelf, she gasped. "They're gone!" She rummaged through the books. Then she tipped them off the shelf and went through everything on the floor. "Even the note from last night is gone!" she cried. "Someone's been in this room!"

Sam watched calmly. *Good. Now I won't have parents messing up my case.*

Beth helped Jennie search the room from top to bottom, but the notes had disappeared.

"Someone stole them!" Beth exclaimed.

"The ghost took them. If we can't show them to anybody, nobody will ever believe us," said Jennie. "He's thought of everything."

Sam hummed happily to herself.

After breakfast, Jennie, Beth and Sam looked for the cellar stairs, but they couldn't find any. "Maybe they're outside," said Jennie. "Like at my grandma's house."

"Let's look," said Beth, leading the way out.

Creeping around the edge of the house, they kept close to the wall so that no one could see them from the windows. They could feel the ghost everywhere.

At one corner of the house Sam stopped and sniffed at some dead weeds and bricks. Very faintly she caught that musty smell again. *Hey! It's here. I smell the cellar.*

"Sam found the cellar!"

Over here!

"We'd better move these bricks." Jennie

looked at the rubble. She pulled at a brick and lifted it carefully. Underneath wriggled snails and slugs. "Ugh."

Bit by bit they moved the debris until weathered gray boards appeared.

"Another door!" cried Beth.

Open it!

Beth tugged at the door. To her surprise, it moved easily. "It doesn't seem as if it's been shut very long," she said in a puzzled voice.

Who cares! Get it open!

When the girls opened the trap door, the familiar dank smell wafted out to them. With Sam in the lead, they crept down the mossy stairs. On the bottom step, they crouched and stared into the stone cellar. It was dim and dark and forbidding.

"I can't see the sword." Beth peered into the darkness.

"I — I wonder if he killed people with it." Jennie chewed her lip nervously.

"I bet the ghost is watching us," said Beth in a small voice, her eyes darting around fearfully.

"I d-d-don't think we should go in," Jennie stammered.

"Me neither."

We need to search the place.

"It's dangerous, Sam," whispered Jennie.

Sam snorted. *He's in there somewhere. And so is the treasure.*

Jennie was firm. "We're not going in, Sam."

Sam stared at Jennie in disbelief. Without another word, Sam marched into the dimness. Ignoring the girls, she sniffed around the floor. In the darkest part of the cellar, her toenail struck something.

Groping with her paw, Sam felt something sticking out of the dirt. She licked at it and discovered it was made of wood. It felt like the corner of something. *A treasure chest! I've found it!*

Sam started digging. *It's the treasure! Help me!*

"Sam's found the treasure!" Jennie cried. "She needs help."

Dirt flew from Sam's paws. Jennie and Beth ran over to Sam and knelt down to scrape with their fingernails. As they dug, a corner appeared out of the dirt.

It's a money box! Sam dug frantically.

Jennie and Beth scraped and scraped. Their fingers hurt, but they didn't slow down. They pulled at it. It was only a piece of wood.

Drat!

Slam! Suddenly, they were plunged into blackness.

Deep, deep darkness surrounded them as if they had been thrown to the bottom of a pit.

Beth's voice echoed in the inky blackness. "He slammed the door."

Jennie whispered, "M-m-maybe it just fell … Maybe …" Her voice trailed off.

Sam's growl filled the dark cellar. Jennie felt in her pocket for the flashlight and switched it on. Their faces were chalk white.

Jennie's lower lip trembled. "M-maybe it was the wind." Her scalp tingled with fear.

"Let's get out of here." Beth's voice shook.

Following the light from the flashlight, Jennie and Beth crept back up the stairs. They pushed at the trap door. It didn't move.

"Grrrrr."

"Push harder," hissed Jennie, feeling panic rise in her chest.

They pushed as hard as they could, but the door wouldn't budge.

"Harder," wheezed Beth.

Nothing happened.

They were trapped.

19. Sam Is a Hero

The three friends crouched on the stairs. The only sound was the thudding of their hearts.

"M-m-my parents are going to be really sorry they didn't believe in that g-ghost," squeaked Jennie.

"Everybody will be sad, but we'll be in our coffins," sniffled Beth.

Jennie started to cry. "What do ghosts do to their prisoners?"

"I don't know."

They both threw their arms around Sam and buried their faces in her fur. They waited to feel the ghost's icy hands on their necks.

Gently, Sam licked their faces. *I'm sorry,*

Jennie. It's my fault. I'll dig us out. I'll — Wait a minute.

Sam pushed her hairy face in front of Jennie's and stared. *Stop crying.*

"W-What?" stammered Jennie through her tears.

There's a way out of here. Remember? The tunnel!

Relief spread over Jennie's tearstained face. "We're not trapped!" she hiccuped. "We forgot about the tunnel!"

"The tunnel!" muttered Beth, fiercely wiping tears from her cheeks. "How could we be so stupid?"

Everybody stop blubbering. We're out of here!

Huddling together, they followed the light back through the cellar. Fearfully, Jennie shone her flashlight over the stone walls. When it lit up one corner, they all gasped.

"That's not a sword!" whispered Jennie.

"It's an old rake!" giggled Beth nervously. "You were wrong, Sam."

So, nobody's perfect. Sam shoved at Jennie's leg. *Come on. We're leaving.*

Jennie's light moved over the stone walls again. The door to the tunnel was just as they remembered it. With all their strength, Jennie and Beth pushed on it.

Finally the door began to move. It creaked open into the tunnel.

They scrambled through the opening and down the narrow passageway. Down, down, down they followed the bobbing light.

"Hurry," panted Beth. "He's going to catch us!"

"He's right behind us!" wheezed Jennie, feeling the ghost's icy breath on her back.

Sam felt as if One-Eye was grabbing her fur. She could hear his soft ghostly moans. *He wants to lock us in! Hurry!*

At last they came to the door on the beach. It wouldn't budge. "Oh no!" cried Beth, banging on the door. "The latch on the outside must have clicked shut!"

One-Eye was coming. Closer … Closer …

There's got to be a way out. Sam clawed frantically at the dirt. *I'll dig under this door.*

"Sam's going to dig," whispered Jennie.

Loose sand flew beneath Sam's feet.

I'm getting us out!

Too terrified to move, Jennie and Beth flattened themselves against the tunnel wall. They could hear One-Eye moaning.

"I think he's laughing," said Beth in a tiny voice. "He's got us now."

Not yet he doesn't! Sam dug like a wild thing.

Daylight peeked from under the door. Sam's feet flew. The patch of light got bigger. Sam stuck her head under the door, backed out and started digging again. Dirt sprayed over the girls.

At last Sam got down and wriggled under the door. *Follow me! Get out before it's too late!*

Jennie lay flat. "Come on, Beth! Hurry!" She stuck her head through the space under the door and wriggled. Beth was right behind her.

Through the branches they burst into the daylight. Blinking, they scrambled onto the empty beach.

"We're out!" they cried. "Sam, you're a hero!"

Whew! Sam tugged at the twigs in her fur. *That was a close one.*

Half laughing and half crying, Jennie and Beth threw themselves on the sand.

Sam stood up and shook herself. She stared at Jennie intently.

So, how about a snack?

When they got to their bedroom, the door slammed behind them.

Beth jumped. "That slam is getting louder."

"He's really mad." Jennie gulped.

Of course he's mad. He didn't catch us. As Sam shook herself, she sprayed leaves and sand everywhere. Then she jumped on the bed and settled her head on a pillow. In her mind, she saw One-Eye screaming and shaking his fist. His evil face was contorted with fury. *Tough luck, One-Eye. You didn't get us!*

"We made it!" Jennie's brown hair was full of twigs, and her hands and legs were filthy.

Beth looked at her muddy fingernails and dirty knees. "We're a mess," she said, yanking sticks from her red curls. "Good thing your family's in the front garden."

There's nothing to worry about. Sam stretched out. *Relax.*

"Nothing to worry about!" exclaimed Jennie.

Beth gasped. "Nothing to worry about! Only a killer ghost trying to trap us!"

Well, maybe there were a few tense moments. But we're out, so forget it. Sam fixed the girls with a hard stare. *We've got to find the treasure. Let's see the treasure.*

Jennie sighed. "Sam still wants to find the treasure."

How about it? Let's see if Briggsy's got it.

20. Spying on Briggsy

That night Jennie, Beth and Sam waited until it was dark and the family was watching television. Letting themselves quietly out of the house, they made their way across the lawn toward the caretaker's cottage. Shadows moved over the grass. Overhead, the black trees whispered in the night breeze.

As they stole through the night, their scalps prickled. They could feel the ghost hovering on the air.

"I wonder what Briggsy does in there," whispered Beth. "She's so weird."

Jennie nodded. "I think Sam's right. I think she takes orders from the ghost."

"She sure looks spooky."

I bet Old One-Eye comes tonight.

Jennie shuddered. "I don't really want to see the ghost, Sam."

Relax. I have —

"I know," interrupted Jennie. "You have great teeth."

When they got close to the cottage, they fell silent. Bright windows threw patches of light on the inky grass. Together they circled the light and flattened themselves against the wall of the little house.

Beth motioned to an open patio door. Falling to their hands and knees, they crept along the wall. Then they stopped and listened. There was only the sound of a television.

"Ready?" mouthed Beth. Jennie nodded.

Jennie and Beth leaned slowly around the door frame to look through the screen. Carefully they leaned a little more ... and a little more ... At last they could see in.

Briggsy was sitting in the living room watching television. Her bare feet were on a footstool. Her spectacles had slid down to the end of her nose.

Flowered couches, bookcases and a fireplace made the small room cozy. All over the walls were paintings of the beach, the house and the neighboring countryside.

Jennie and Beth held their breath and watched. After a few minutes, Briggsy stood up and stretched. She turned off the television. She looked around the room, picking up newspapers and books, plumping up pillows and tidying. She stretched again and yawned.

Behind the girls, Sam jostled. *I can't see. Let me in.*

They watched Briggsy take off her glasses. Then Briggsy reached up, grabbed her bun and pulled. Beth and Jennie gasped. Off it came. And out tumbled long silky brown hair.

I can't see. Sam shoved them. *You are the biggest hogs in the world. Let me in there!*

But Jennie wasn't listening. Briggsy's long hair fell around her wrinkled face and her white eyebrows. She started to unbutton the front of her baggy housekeeper's dress.

Let me see! Sam pushed at them. *I can't believe how selfish you are!*

Briggsy stepped out of her baggy dress. She was wearing shorts and a top. And she was slim.

I can't see!

Then Briggsy did an amazing thing. First she pulled off each white eyebrow. Next she leaned over and grabbed at the edges of her face. Her wrinkles peeled off. When she raised her head, she didn't look anything like the scowly old housekeeper who had terrified them.

Jennie and Beth gasped again. Briggsy was young and pretty!

I've had it! Let me see or I'm going to bite somebody! Sam pushed again.

Jennie and Beth tried to hold on to the door frame.

"Oh no!" shrieked Beth as Sam butted her from behind.

"Yikes!" screamed Jennie.

Through the patio-door screen they crashed! With Sam on top, the girls sprawled in the doorway, covered with bits of shredded screen.

Briggsy screamed.

Whoops. Maybe I pushed too hard.

21. The Mystery of the Notes

Briggsy stood over them, hands on her hips.

"Grrrrr."

"Grrr yourself!" yelled Briggsy. "What do you kids think you're doing?"

"Ummmm," gulped Beth.

"Ah-ah-ah-ah," stammered Jennie.

Sam stared at Briggsy. She looked at the spectacles on the coffee table and the long brown hair around Briggsy's shoulders. She looked at Briggsy's smooth skin and brown eyebrows. *Hmm ...*

"This is outrageous!" screamed Briggsy.

Jennie turned bright pink. Beth's face flushed as red as her hair.

"You rotten little snoops!" Briggsy stamped her foot with rage. "I demand an explanation!"

"Ummmm," stammered Beth. "Ugh-gh-gh."

"Errrrr," stuttered Jennie.

Sam scowled. *We're the ones who demand an explanation. Why does Briggsy wear a disguise? Ask her.*

"Argh," choked Jennie, her tongue sticking to her dry mouth.

Sam bumped Jennie. *Speak up! Find out why she dresses like that.*

"Ahhhh." Jennie's face flushed.

"This better be good!" screeched Briggsy. "Sit right there and tell me what's going on."

Jennie and Beth perched on the edge of the sofa. Beth felt hot and sweaty. Jennie felt sick.

"Now!" shouted Briggsy. "Why were you spying on me?"

Sam glared at Briggsy. *Never mind us. What are you up to?*

Jennie opened her mouth and then shut it. It was no use. Her tongue wouldn't work.

Briggsy sat in a chair and folded her arms.

"Nobody leaves until I get some answers."

Tell her. We might find out something.

When Jennie finally spoke, her voice squeaked. "W-we were trying to see the ghost."

Briggsy glared. "You think there's a ghost here?"

The girls nodded.

Briggsy rolled her eyes to the ceiling. "The whole world thinks there's a ghost here!" She started to pace. "Do you have any idea how sick I am of this ghost story?"

"Ummm. N-n-no," stammered Jennie.

"So many people come looking for this ridiculous ghost. They're ruining my life!" She waved wildly toward the pictures on the walls. "I'm an artist!" she shrieked. "I need to be left alone to paint!"

Briggsy put her hands on her hips again. "Why were you spying on me? What do I have to do with a ghost?"

Beth cleared her throat. "We were trying to find his treasure … since he was a pirate …" Her voice trailed off under Briggsy's hard stare.

All the veins stood out on Briggsy's neck. "Treasure!" she screamed. "Do you mean people are going to be snooping around looking for treasure now?"

Tell her we're not answering any more questions. Ask her why she wears a disguise.

Beth chewed her fingernails. "We knew the ghost was Captain Briggs, so we were looking for his pirate treasure."

"That's the stupidest thing I've ever heard!"

Sam drew herself up proudly. *Watch who you're calling stupid.*

Briggsy looked at them long and hard. "Captain Percival Briggs was flat broke. I'm related to the only pirate in the world without a treasure. He was a failure – a flop."

She's trying to throw us off the trail.

Jennie and Beth sat very still.

You can't fool us, Briggsy. There's a big treasure around here, and we're going to get it.

Briggsy looked steadily at the girls. "Look, I'm sorry I yelled so much, but I'm telling the truth. There is no treasure."

That's just the kind of thing an old bat would say.

Jennie swallowed. "A-a-are you sure?"

"Absolutely sure."

"Why is there a tunnel if there's no treasure?" asked Beth bravely.

"Oh that!" Briggsy snorted. "In the 1920s, smugglers hid liquor in that tunnel." She sighed. "I come from a long line of criminals. And none of them made any money."

Ask her why she dresses in that disguise.

"E-e-excuse me, Mrs. Briggs," said Jennie nervously. "Why do you wear that disguise?"

Mrs. Briggs flushed. "I was trying to scare you away. I hate people in my house! I only rent it when I need money."

"So you wanted to get rid of us!" Beth watched Briggsy carefully.

"I wanted you out the minute you started to snoop! I hate spies." She glowered at them. "Do you know that this house is on a national tour of historic spots? Busloads of people come here to snoop."

"So that's why you dress up?" asked Beth.

"Of course it's why!" snapped Briggsy. "I thought if I looked grumpy enough, people might leave me alone."

Briggsy started to pace again. "But it doesn't work! They get out of the bus and they tramp all over my yard. They walk right up on the porch and ask to see the ghost." She waved her arms and screamed. "There is no ghost!"

Briggsy paused for breath. "I don't have a minute's peace. And I need peace and quiet to paint."

Jennie and Beth didn't know what to say.

Tell this old bat we heard the ghost with our own ears.

"We heard the ghost in the attic," said Jennie. "He sneaks around up there."

"There are squirrels in that attic!" cried Mrs. Briggs. "They make a lot of noise and they do a lot of damage." She glared at them. "Just like kids."

"The bedroom door slams all the time," added Beth stubbornly.

Briggsy looked at Beth as if she was very, very

stupid. "The floor in that hall is slanted. That's why the door slams."

Sam was getting grumpy. *Who wrote the notes if there's no ghost?*

Jennie looked up at Mrs. Briggs. "Someone put notes under our door. If there's no ghost, who wrote them?" she asked politely.

Mrs. Briggs flushed.

Look at her face!

Jennie nudged Beth.

She wrote them!

They all stared at Mrs. Briggs.

Mrs. Briggs didn't flinch. She thrust out her jaw. "I can't stand snoops. I'm an artist. I need peace and quiet."

Beth gasped. "You wrote them!"

"You wanted to scare us away!" Jennie chimed in.

Ha! I was right! She really is an old bat — just like I thought.

22. One-Eye Says Good-bye

The next morning, Sam, Jennie and Beth moped around the bedroom. Nobody felt like getting up.

Sam was disgusted. *No ghost. No treasure. Only a weirdo in a Halloween costume.* She cocked her head. *Better not tell your parents about Briggsy. They'll know we've been spying.*

"I was sure there was a ghost," sighed Jennie.

"So was I," echoed Beth.

If there's no ghost I won't get my picture in the newspaper.

Jennie patted Sam gently. "Poor Sam. You really want to be famous, don't you?"

Suddenly Sam sat up. *Wait a minute. What about*

that kid on the beach? The kid who was digging.

"Yeah," said Jennie. "Liam was looking for treasure. Wasn't he, Beth?"

Beth jumped to her feet. "He sure was! Let's go to the village and see if we can find him. Maybe Briggsy lied about everything."

Sam's head whipped up. *Of course she lied. She wants us off the case!*

Quickly the girls pulled on shorts and T-shirts and ran downstairs. In minutes, they were on their bikes, heading toward town.

I've seen Liam in the park, puffed Sam.

"Good," said Jennie. "We'll look there first."

They had just stopped at a corner when they saw Liam.

"Wait a minute!" yelled Beth as they pedaled hard to catch up.

"Wait up! We need to ask you something!" hollered Jennie.

Sam decided to be friendly. Wiggling around Liam's legs, she licked his hand.

"I hate dog slobber," Liam muttered.

Better than kid slobber. Sam licked harder.

"Yuck!" Liam snatched his hand away.

Blech! The disgusting things a clever detective has to do.

Liam scowled at the girls. "I suppose you want to steal more maps?"

Beth and Jennie blushed. "No. We need to ask you something."

"So, ask."

"We've been looking for Captain Briggs' treasure," began Beth.

"Treasure? Not that again."

"The same treasure you're looking for," said Beth firmly.

"I'm not looking for treasure!"

"What about the treasure map we found?" asked Jennie.

Liam stared at them as if they had lost their minds. "Treasure map? It was a fossil map. I've been looking for fossils."

"Fossils?" Beth cried.

What's a fossil?

"You mean old bones stuck in rocks?" asked Jennie.

Liam looked at her as if she was an idiot. "I collect fossils. That beach is a great place to find them."

"Oh."

When Liam thought about his fossils, he cheered up. "I could show you my collection. I've got a great trilobite and an ichthyosaurus skull and an archaeopteryx claw. Want to see them?"

Sam rolled her eyes. *Definitely not my idea of a good time.*

"Uh, maybe later." Jennie tried to sound polite.

Beth eyed Liam closely. "You never thought there was a treasure?"

Liam shook his head. "Of course not."

"But," tried Beth, "the ghost was a pirate, so he must have treasure."

"There's no treasure," Liam insisted. "Everybody knows that Captain Briggs died poor."

"Are you sure?" Jennie looked at him hard.

"Of course I'm sure. I've lived here all my life. I would know if there was a treasure." Liam turned to go. "Call me if you want to see my fossils. They're the *real* treasures."

Yeah, right! Old rocks. That kid needs to get out more.

"I can't stand Mrs. Briggs any more," complained Jennie's mom. "I'm glad our vacation is almost over."

Jennie's dad sighed. "She's like a black cloud hanging over us. We may as well go home."

"Hurray!" shouted Noel. "I'm going to call Myrna and tell her the good news."

Lucky Myrna.

When they were cleaning their bedroom, Beth found the notes. "Look!" she cried. "Somebody stuffed these notes under the mattress!"

Sam tried to crawl under the bed.

Jennie looked at the notes. They were covered with teeth marks. "Sam didn't want me to show the notes to my parents, remember?"

Sam squished herself farther under the bed. *People always blame dogs.*

Jennie leaned down and looked under the bed. "There's no use hiding, Sam. We know you hid the notes." She sat down on the bed. "Not that it matters. Those notes weren't from the ghost. They were from Briggsy."

I hope a big busload of people comes today. I hope they tramp on her gardens and stomp all over her house.

Jennie ripped the notes into little shreds. "I think Briggsy told us the truth, Beth. I don't think there's a ghost here."

"Liam probably said the house is haunted just because it's old," added Beth glumly.

Under the bed, Sam heaved an enormous sigh. *Great. Now my partners are giving up.*

After everyone was asleep that night, Sam sneaked outside. For a long time, she sat on the back lawn, looking out at the shimmering lake.

Ghostly noises whispered through the trees. Moonlight touched her white fur and made it gleam.

In the still night, Sam listened. She heard scratching sounds from the attic above her. She heard the swoosh of a boat on the lake.

In her mind, Sam saw a pirate ship filled with treasure and manned by cutthroats. She saw pirates unload the treasure chest, row it to shore and carry it into the tunnel. Along the tunnel walls flickered the light from burning torches. One-Eye led the way, laughing about how well they would hide this treasure. No one would ever find it.

Sam sighed and went through the bushes toward the caretaker's cottage. There were no lights on. Everything was silent. Everything was still.

Sam sniffed at the windows. She could faintly smell Briggsy's hairspray. At the last window, she paused. From somewhere inside the house she could hear a low voice.

"Imagine those kids looking for pirate

treasure." It was Briggsy. "How stupid can you get!"

So she does talk to One-Eye after all.

Then Briggsy spoke again. "The nerve of those kids."

Sam listened, but she couldn't hear anyone answer. *I guess I can't hear One-Eye because he's a ghost.*

"I wonder if their parents know what brats they have," muttered Briggsy.

Sam cocked her head, but she couldn't make out anything else.

Sam sat in the shadows until the talking stopped, and the night was silent again. For a long time Sam listened. At last, stiff from the damp night, she stood up to go home.

As she turned back to the house, something caught her eye. There was a shape in the trees ahead. Sam squinted to get a better look. She was sure it was One-Eye himself. His white teeth gleamed at her. His sword glinted in the moonlight. He threw back his head and laughed and laughed.

Then he disappeared.

In the small attic window, Sam saw a misty shimmer of white, and she heard the laugh again. Instantly the shape was gone.

Briggsy is lying about everything. And I'm the only one smart enough to know it.

The family was busy packing the car. To Sam's disgust, Jennie and Beth said they were finished with the mystery. No matter how much Sam argued, they said there was no ghost.

Sam spent every last minute sniffing around to see if she could find something. Twice she looked up to see Briggsy watching her. *You are a sneaky old bat,* thought Sam grimly as she sniffed.

It was time to leave. Beth's parents arrived and whisked her away. Before Sam knew it, she found herself bundled into the car beside Jennie.

"Well, we had a pretty good holiday," said Mr. Levinsky as he pulled out of the driveway.

"It would have been lovely," agreed Mrs. Levinsky, "except for that nasty Mrs. Briggs. She doesn't have to worry about us renting again."

Noel started to complain about how much he had hated it, but Sam tuned him out. *Blah blah blah.*

Wistfully, Sam looked out the car window as they turned away from the house. Suddenly the back of her neck tingled. There it was! A shimmer of white against the attic window!

Yes! There it is again! thought Sam excitedly as the car sped up. She wriggled and craned her neck to look back at the house. Very faintly, she could hear One-Eye laughing. *This settles it! I'm coming back.*

As the car rolled along, Sam hummed to herself. *Somehow ... someday ... I'm coming back. I'm going to get a close look at that ghost if it's the last thing I do ...*